LOVE SPELL
HOW TO WISH ON A STAR
dreams
oil
newt

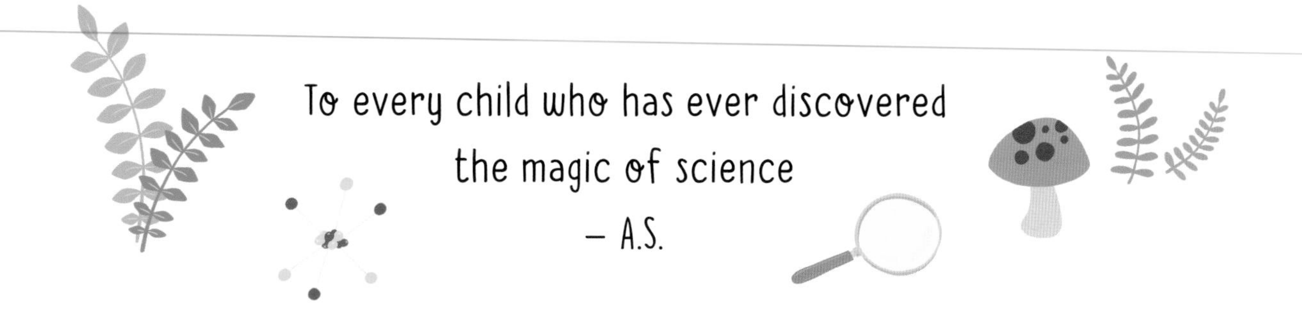

To every child who has ever discovered
the magic of science
– A.S.

Tundra Books, an imprint of Penguin Random House Canada Young Readers, a Penguin Random House Company

Library and Archives Canada Cataloguing in Publication

Spires, Ashley, 1978-, author, illustrator
Fairy science / [written and illustrated by] Ashley Spires.

(Fairy science ; 1)
Issued in print and electronic formats.
ISBN 978-0-7352-6425-0 (hardcover).--ISBN 978-0-7352-6426-7 (EPUB)

I. Title.
PS8637.P57F35 2019 jC813'.6 C2018-904494-2
C2018-904495-0

Published simultaneously in the United States of America by Crown Books for Young Readers, an imprint of Penguin Random House LLC, New York

Edited by Phoebe Yeh and Tara Walker
The artwork in this book was rendered digitally after wishing on a star, planting it in soil and giving it plenty of sunlight.

Printed and bound in China

www.penguinrandomhouse.ca

1 2 3 4 5 23 22 21 20 19

Ashley Spires

tundra

Esther does not believe in magic.

This is unusual because Esther is a fairy, and fairies are all about magic.

They use magic wands, and they mix magic potions.
Some fairies even make magical fairy dust.

Esther is pretty sure that's just dandruff.

She is the only fairy in Pixieville who believes in science.

Esther prefers facts, data, and hard evidence to wishing on stars.

LABORATORY!
ESTHER'S ROOM
PERIODIC TABLE OF THE ELEMENTS

Unfortunately, the only thing they teach in fairy school is magic. Class is very frustrating for Esther.

Fairies were born when a drop of rain passed through a rainbow and landed on a flower bud. When the flower bloomed, the first fairy took flight!

And for Ms. Pelly Petal.

Esther can't help observing the world differently from everyone else. Where other fairies see a path to hidden gold, Esther sees light and water colliding.

Follow the rainbow!

The water helps us see all the colors that are hidden in the sunlight! That's dispersion.

Where they see a dangerous omen, she sees condensation.

Where they see faces of the spirits, she sees erosion.

Esther can't wait to teach the scientific method to her fairymates.

Do experiments!
Study the results!
Draw a conclusion!
EUREKA!
Or you could just do magic.

She shows them the periodic table.

She even demonstrates gravity!
WHEEEEEEEEEE!
Gravity is why things fall down instead of up!
But WE can go up, so we must be magic!

THEY JUST DON'T GET IT!

That was definitely gravity.

And there is definitely something wrong with this tree.

The fairies do their best to help. They cast spells.

They make magic talismans.

They even do a mystical moonlight dance.

But nothing works. The tree keeps on wilting.

Esther asks a question.

Why is the tree wilting?

She does some research.

WHAT I KNOW ABOUT TREES
1) They have leaves.
2) They have roots.
3) They are pretty.
4) They grow out of dirt.

She makes a hypothesis.

She tries some experiments.

She studies her results.

At last, Esther draws a conclusion!

The tree needs more . . .

SUN!

Sim balla hoo,
Sim balla hee,
I'm doing some magic
To save this tree!

Now she waits for the sun to do its work.

It took a while, but the tree is looking positively perky.

She did it! Esther has proven the power of science!

At least she *thought* she did.

She might not have changed the other fairies' minds . . .
Hip, hip, hooray!
Sigh.

But Esther has inspired some questions.

And that's where every good scientist starts.

LABORATORY!
ESTHER'S ROOM
PERIODIC TABLE OF THE ELEMENTS

ESTHER'S SUN-BEAN EXPERIMENT

Finally, seal up the bag and tape it to a well-lit window. Just like our tree, these plants need sun to grow!
Ta-da!
Once your experiment is set, make a hypothesis about how long you think it will take the seedlings to grow.
This is called germination.
Study your results every day to see how your seeds change and make conclusions about what you see!
That's the scientific method!

2
PERIODIC TABLE OF THE ELEMENTS
NOTES
SODA